FINIST THE FALCON

For Jocelyn, who goes with courage on each new adventure and brings her stories back to us. With special thanks to Galina Savchenko and her family for giving Jocelyn a home in Moscow.

Library of Congress Cataloging-in-Publication Data

Lippert, Meg.
    Finist the falcon: a Russian legend/retold by Meg Lippert;
illustrated by Dave Albers.
        p.   cm.—(Legends of the world)
    Summary: Galya, a merchant's daughter with two unkind sisters,
goes in search of her love Finist the falcon, who is sometimes a bird and
sometimes a fine young man.
        ISBN 0-8167-4025-9 (pbk)
        [1. Fairy tales. 2. Folklore—Russia.] I. Albers, Dave, 1961– , ill.
II. Title.
PZ8.L685Fi   1996
398.2'0947'01—dc20   96-24811

Printed in the United States of America.   ISBN 0-8167-4025-9
10 9 8 7 6 5 4 3 2

FINIST THE FALCON

A RUSSIAN LEGEND

RETOLD BY MEG LIPPERT ILLUSTRATED BY DAVE ALBERS

TROLL

nce, long ago, there lived a merchant who had three daughters. His two elder daughters, Nadia and Svetlana, primped and preened all day long. They made their younger sister, Galya, do all the work around the house.

One day Galya was weeding the garden when a sudden shadow crossed her hand. Looking up, she saw a brilliantly colored falcon alight on a branch right beside her. Never had Galya seen such an unusual bird. She froze, afraid any movement might frighten it away.

"Who are you?" she asked softly. "Have you come to be my friend?"

The falcon's dark eyes reflected her own. It opened its hooked beak and said one word: "Finist." Then it spread its great wings, circled around her three times, and flew off over the forest.

"Finist the Falcon," Galya whispered. "I thought you were only a legend." Galya shaded her eyes and watched the falcon until it was a tiny speck in the sky.

The next day, when the merchant set out for town, he asked his daughters, "What would my beautiful daughters like me to bring them? Satin shoes? Sweets? Perhaps even a handsome young son of a czar?" He laughed.

"Gold earrings for me," said Svetlana.

"Silver for me," said Nadia.

"And diamond ones for you, Galya?" he asked, looking kindly at his youngest daughter.

"My heart desires only one thing, Papa," said Galya. "A feather from Finist the Falcon."

"An unusual request from a most unusual daughter!" said her father with a smile. "I will do what I can."

When Papa arrived in town, he immediately bought two pairs of fancy earrings. But he searched in vain for the special feather. It was nowhere to be found.

At the end of the day, tired and discouraged, Papa slung his bag over his shoulder and started for home. All he could think about was the look of disappointment in Galya's eyes when he told her about the feather. He was so deep in thought that he nearly stumbled over a beggar who sat huddled by the side of the road.

"I'm sorry," said the merchant as he regained his balance. "I was thinking only of my troubles and didn't notice you. Please take this freshly baked loaf of bread in apology for my clumsiness."

"You are kind," said the beggar. "To thank you for your generosity, please accept this small box. Inside is a colored feather that I found in the forest. It is from Finist the Falcon."

Papa was overjoyed. He hurried home with his gifts.

When Svetlana and Nadia got their earrings, they quickly put them on and tossed their heads to hear them jangle. Then they turned and left the room without so much as a thank-you.

"Were you able to find my gift as well, Papa?" asked Galya expectantly.

"I was able to find only this small gift," sighed her father in mock disappointment, as he held out the box. When Galya opened the box, her heart leaped with joy, for there lay the brilliant falcon feather.

"Oh, Papa!" she cried. "You have brought me my heart's desire! Thank you!" She threw her arms around his neck and kissed his bearded cheek.

Later, in her room, Galya once again gently lifted the lid of the box. This time the feather fluttered out with a life of its own. The moment it touched the floor, it became the very falcon that Galya had seen before.

Astonished, she reached out and stroked its soft feathers. "Finist, I believe you have come to be my friend. I will love you and care for you always," she promised. Instantly the bird disappeared, and before her stood the son of a czar clothed in brightly colored velvet.

"Do not be afraid," he said, taking her hands in his own. "I have been searching over land and sea for a maiden who could love me as a falcon, without knowing I am the son of a czar. Because you loved me in my falcon form, I now show you who I am."

The two talked long into the night, and the more they shared, the more they grew to love each other.

At daybreak, Finist said, "Galya, I love you. Will you come away with me and be my bride?" Before she could respond, the door to her room burst open. She spun around as her sisters rushed into her room.

"Where is he?" Nadia screeched.

"We heard a man's voice," added Svetlana.

Galya turned back to Finist, but he was gone. A single colored feather had floated to the floor as the falcon flew out the window. Galya picked up the feather and held it close to her heart.

"Maybe he's hiding in here," said Nadia as she threw open the lid of the chest.

Svetlana thrust a broom handle under the bed. "He's not under here," she said.

They searched everywhere but found no one. "Come on, Svetlana," Nadia said as they left the room. "Galya needs to finish dusting with that special feather duster she's clutching."

Svetlana laughed. "Toss it out and get another," she said over her shoulder. "That's useless. It's got only one feather left!"

That night, while Galya was sleeping, Nadia and Svetlana crouched outside under her window. "I know I heard a man's voice," Nadia whispered. "He must have been talking to her through the window."

"Yes," agreed Svetlana. "He was probably planning to climb in, but when he heard us, he ran away."

"Let's make sure he won't get in tonight," Nadia said. The two sisters sneaked to the edge of the woods and cut piles of long blackberry brambles. Quietly they covered Galya's window with the thick branches and sharp thorns.

"No one will ever be able to get through this window now," Svetlana whispered meanly.

ater that night, Finist the Falcon swooped from the sky straight to the window of his beloved. He didn't see the branches in time. Thorns pierced his neck. Blood spurted onto the windowsill. Broken feathers drifted to the ground.

Wounded and barely able to fly, Finist called to Galya. "Why have you done this to me, my dearest?" he cried. "Have you stopped loving me so soon, or has someone played a cruel trick? I must leave now. If you love me, you must follow me through three times ten countries, to the thrice tenth czardom, which lies at the edge of the sea. On your journey you must wear out three pairs of iron shoes, break three iron walking sticks, and eat three stone loaves. The journey will be long and hard, but you will succeed if you do not give up."

In the middle of the night, Galya awoke. Her room should have been lit by the full moon, but instead it was strangely dark. Feeling her way to the window, she discovered that it was covered with briars. She cut them away and saw, in the moonlight, drops of blood on the windowsill and broken feathers on the ground. "My cruel sisters must have done this," she said to herself. Then she remembered the words of the falcon that she had heard in her dreams, and she wept.

At last, having shed her tears, Galya gathered a few belongings and tied them together into a bundle. Glancing around her room for the last time, she closed the door, whispered farewell to her father, and tiptoed out of the house.

By the side of the path, three long, smooth stones shaped like loaves of bread shone in the moonlight, and she added them to her bundle. Then she hurried down the road to the blacksmith's shop. She knew the blacksmith would arrive at dawn, so she had no time to lose. She pushed open the door and lit the fire herself. She forged three pairs of iron shoes and three iron walking sticks. Just as the first beams of the sun broke through the forest to light her pathway, Galya left some coins for the blacksmith and started on her journey to the thrice tenth czardom.

Day after day Galya walked. Night after night she fell exhausted onto the ground and slept. At first the time went quickly, as she recalled each moment she had shared with Finist the Falcon. But days stretched into weeks, and weeks lengthened into months. With the coming of autumn, the warm summer afternoons gave way to cool days and cold nights.

Galya could feel the rocks through the holes in her iron shoes. One iron walking stick had cracked. Then, one day, just as she was finishing the last bite of a stone loaf, she thought she heard someone singing. Making her way slowly up the path, Galya rounded a bend and saw an old woman with snow white hair seated by the door of a hut. The woman was spinning thread from ordinary flax with a silver distaff and a golden spindle. Galya stared in astonishment, for the spun thread was pure gold. Without looking up, the woman finished her song and addressed Galya.

"Hello, my child."

"Hello, Babushka," said Galya. "I am searching for my love, Finist the Falcon. Do you know where I may find him?"

"I have heard he has just proposed marriage to the daughter of a czar who lives in a country far away over the mountains, twice ten lands from here."

The old woman tossed a ball of the golden thread into the forest. "Follow this ball wherever it rolls," she said. "It will lead you on the shortest path to my elder sister. Perhaps she can direct you further." The old woman gave Galya the silver distaff and the golden spindle. "You may need these," she said. "Go with courage. May you find your heart's desire."

Galya thanked the old woman and set out to follow the ball.

ver mountains and through streams the ball rolled, and wherever it led, Galya followed. She dreamed of Finist at night and spoke her thoughts aloud as she traveled during the day. "Do you still love me, Finist?" she cried. "Or have you forgotten me?"

Days and weeks and months wore on. Winter winds blew frigid, and snow blanketed the forest. Weariness weighed as heavily on Galya as the iron shoes on her feet. Without the ball she would have been utterly lost. Her second pair of iron shoes had worn thin, and her second iron walking stick had split in two. As she swallowed the last bit of her second stone loaf, she thought she heard a song.

The ball led her into a clearing in the forest and stopped before a hut where an old woman with a hooked nose sat twirling a golden egg on a silver dish. Galya watched in amazement. Every time the egg turned once around, another golden egg appeared. The old woman added each new egg to the growing heap of golden eggs beside her. Without looking up, the woman greeted Galya.

"Hello, my child."

"Hello, Babushka," said Galya. "I am searching for my love, Finist the Falcon. I must see him before he marries the czar's daughter."

"Then you must make haste. You still have ten more lands to cross. My elder sister lives at the edge of the thrice tenth czardom. She can direct you further." The old woman gave Galya the egg and the dish. "Go with courage," she said. "May you find your heart's desire."

Galya thanked the old woman. Filled with new hope, she ran to catch up with the ball.

Galya traveled until she thought she could go no farther. As the moon waxed and waned, the snows melted and turned to heavy mud. With each footstep, her iron shoes sank deeper into the muck. She felt she would soon be swallowed up by the earth itself.

"Finist, my love," she cried. "Will I ever find you?" Only the lonely wind answered her.

She hardly noticed that her iron shoes were once again worn through, her last iron walking stick had long since broken, and just the tiniest morsel of her third stone loaf remained. As darkness fell, she swallowed the last bite and saw that the ball had stopped beside an old woman with only one eye who sat in front of a hut. She held a golden embroidery frame on her lap. Galya stared in wonder as a golden needle sewed shining pictures in the fabric with golden thread. The needle sewed all by itself.

"Hello, my child."

"Hello, Babushka," said Galya.

"Come in and rest. The morning is wiser than the evening." The old woman took Galya by the hand and welcomed her inside. There she bathed her and washed the mud from her hair. She prepared hot borscht and fresh bread, and Galya ate hungrily. She had forgotten how delicious beet soup and crusty bread could taste. She slept peacefully until the sun rose.

"Thank you, Babushka," said Galya. "I must go now. I am searching for my love, Finist the Falcon, who is betrothed to a czar's daughter. Can you help me?"

"Follow the golden ball over the mountain to the next czardom. Wherever it stops, sit down and spin. When the czar's daughter sees you and asks to buy your spindle and distaff, tell her you will give them to her only if you can visit one night with Finist the Falcon."

Galya thanked the old woman and turned to leave, but the old woman put her hand on Galya's arm. She offered Galya the embroidery frame and the needle. "Go with courage," she said. "May you find your heart's desire."

Galya smiled her thanks and hastened after the rolling ball.

alya climbed steeply hour after hour. When it got too dark to see the ball ahead of her, she stopped to sleep until the sky lightened. Day after day she climbed. The days grew longer and warmer. Sweet berries nourished her, and cool spring water refreshed her.

At last Galya reached the crest of the mountain. Beneath her was a wide valley, and beyond was the sea. On the shore was a white palace with golden domes. Galya paused a moment to catch her breath before starting down the path after the swiftly rolling ball. Her bare feet felt so light, she seemed to fly down the mountain.

Nearing her true love at last, she was too excited to sleep more than a few hours at a time. After the sun set, she followed the golden ball by the light of the moon. Several days later she reached the palace. The ball rolled past the gate and stopped at the seashore.

Galya sat down on the sand, took out the silver distaff and the golden spindle, and began spinning flax into golden thread. Soon the czar's daughter came along with all her maids and servants. "Sell me your distaff and spindle," the czar's daughter said. "I will have a wedding dress of gold."

"They are not for sale," Galya said. "But I will give them to you if I may visit one night with Finist the Falcon."

The czar's daughter readily agreed, for she was greedy and deceitful. "What a stupid girl," she said to herself. "I have only to give him a sleeping potion with his supper and he will not wake up all night. Her little visit will be in silence!"

That evening the czar's daughter took the distaff and spindle from Galya and led her to the room where Finist slept. "I will be back for you in the morning," she said.

Galya called to Finist: "I am here, my love. Why do you not wake up? My wicked sisters plotted against us. I crossed thrice ten lands searching for you. I traveled through summer, autumn, winter, and spring. I wore out three pairs of iron shoes, broke three iron walking sticks, and ate three stone loaves. To see you now, I traded my distaff and spindle that spin flax into gold, because the czar's daughter wanted a wedding dress of gold. When the sun rises, I must go. Open your eyes, my love."

All night Galya talked to him. He heard her in his dreams, but he could not wake up.

The next afternoon Galya again sat by the seashore. This time she twirled the golden egg on the silver dish and piled golden eggs on the ground beside her. The czar's daughter came along and said, "What will you take for those eggs and that dish? With golden eggs I can buy a diamond necklace for my wedding."

"They are not for sale," Galya answered. "But I will trade them for another visit with Finist."

"Agreed!" exclaimed the czar's daughter, thinking the girl must be quite foolish. "She never even suspected that I gave him a sleeping potion. Another sleeping potion will take care of him tonight."

That evening, in exchange for the eggs and the dish, the czar's daughter again led Galya to Finist's room. Again Galya told Finist her story. All night long she spoke to him. Although he heard her, he could not wake up.

The third afternoon, Galya sat by the seashore with the golden embroidery frame on her lap. The needle flew up and down by itself. Shimmering pictures appeared on the cloth. The czar's daughter saw this and was awestruck.

"With that frame I can have a magnificent wedding jacket embroidered for my betrothed," she said. "That needle is so fast, it will be finished tomorrow, just in time for our wedding. What will you take for it?"

"You may have it in exchange for one more visit with Finist," said Galya.

"Done!" the czar's daughter shouted, and she took the embroidery frame and the needle back to the palace with her.

That evening the czar's daughter gave Finist a sleeping potion even stronger than those she had given him the two nights before. Then she led Galya to his room.

Galya shook her beloved and called to him over and over. When she noticed the darkness fading, she realized her time with Finist would soon be over forever. She began to weep as she told him once more of her journey, and of her bargains with the czar's daughter. As she leaned over him, a single tear fell on his cheek. His eyes flew open.

"My love! You have
come at last! I thought you
were just in my dreams," he
exclaimed. "While I slept I heard the
story of your long, hard journey, and of the
czar's deceitful daughter. You, Galya, are the one I
love. You have come just in time, for my wedding was to
be today at noon. But now I have a different bride." He smiled
tenderly. "The czar's daughter sold my hours for gold and silver, but you
sought me over thrice ten lands."

At this moment the czar's daughter opened the door to fetch Galya. The
czar's daughter was furious when she saw Finist awake. She rushed at Galya
and raged, "Get out, you wretch."

Instantly Finist turned into a falcon and swept Galya out of reach of the czar's daughter. Together they flew out the window. They soared over the mountains and flew to Finist's own czardom, where he took her in his arms and kissed her.

"You are my own true bride," he said. "Now our wedding will be celebrated by both our families and all the people of this land." So it was, and if they haven't stopped celebrating yet, then they are celebrating still.

Russia is the largest country in the world. It stretches from Europe across Asia to the Pacific Ocean and covers an area almost twice as large as the United States. According to a Russian proverb: "Russia is not a country; it is a world." Many different cultural groups live in Russia, in regions ranging from snow-capped mountains to dry salt flats below sea level. Russia has rich natural resources including mineral deposits, dense forests, fertile soil, and water power.

Throughout the ages, the people of Russia have loved to listen to fairy tales. It is said that one ruler, who lived over 400 years ago, Ivan IV, had three old, blind storytellers who told him fairy tales every night before he went to sleep. For generations Russian fairy tales were preserved by people who told them to one another. In fact, the first collection of Russian fairy tales in Russian was not published until 150 years ago. Today Russians carry on their tradition of storytelling in their schools as well as in their families.

If you go to Russia, you may use some of the Russian words in this book. A *babushka* is a grandmother. *Borscht* is tasty beet soup, often served with sour cream and black rye bread. *Czar* is the Russian word for king or emperor.